THE TAILYPO

for Adam and Danielle

Clarion Books

a Houghton Mifflin Company imprint

215 Park Avenue South, New York, NY 10003

Text copyright © 1977 by Joanna Galdone

Illustrations copyright © 1977 by Paul Galdone

Printed in the USA

Library of Congress Cataloging in Publication Data

Galdone, Joanna.   The tailypo.

Summary: A strange varmint haunts the woodsman who lopped off its tail.

[1. Folklore—United States] I. Galdone, Paul. II. Title.

PZ8.1.G14Tail   [398.2]   [E]   77-23289

RNF ISBN 0-395-28809-6

PAP ISBN 0-395-30084-3

(previously published by The Seabury Press under

ISBN 0-8164-3191-4)

WOZ 20 19 18 17

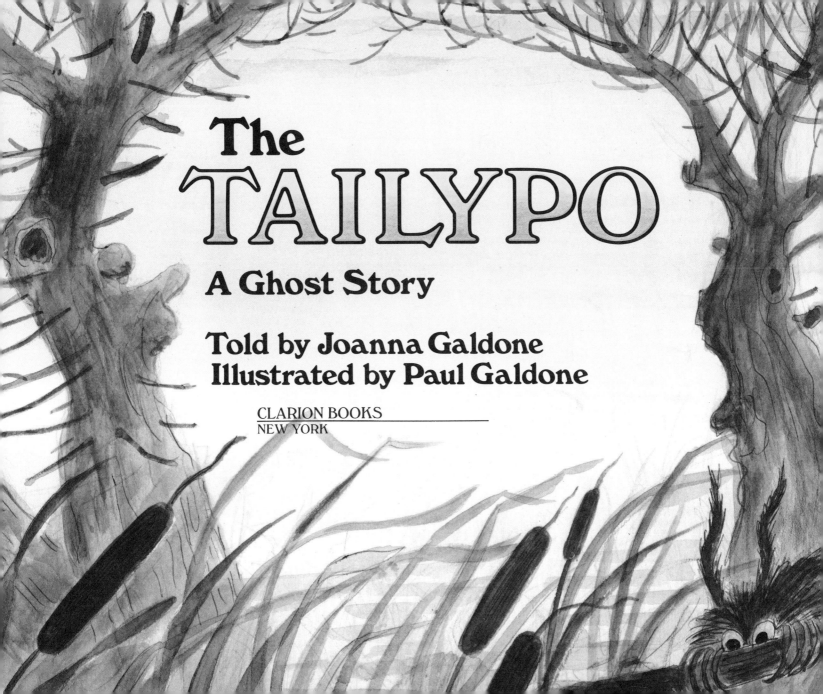

The TAILYPO

A Ghost Story

Told by Joanna Galdone
Illustrated by Paul Galdone

CLARION BOOKS
NEW YORK

long time ago an old man lived by himself
in the deep, big woods. His cabin had only one room,
and that room was his parlor, his bedroom, his dining room
and his kitchen, too.

The old man had three dogs. One was called Uno,
one was called Ino, and one was called Cumptico-Calico.

One day the man decided to go hunting to catch something
for his supper. "Here, here, here!" he shouted to his dogs,
and they came bounding off the porch, eager for a chase.

After many hours of hunting, the wind began to blow hard
from the valley. "It'll be dark soon," the old man said,
"and all we've caught is this skinny rabbit."
He headed home, afraid he might go to bed hungry that night.

The old man was still hungry, so he took that big, long tail, cooked it, and ate it. After that, he stuffed up the crack in the wall and went to bed.

The old man cooked and ate the rabbit and gave the bones to the dogs. Then he leaned back in his chair and watched the moon as it rose up big and full. The wind whistled around the cabin.

Just as the old man was about to doze off,
a most curious creature crept through a crack between the logs in the wall.
It had a BIG, LONG, FURRY TAIL.

As soon as the old man saw the varmint he reached
for his hatchet, and with one lick he cut its tail off!
Before the man could raise his hatchet a second time,
the creature slipped out through the crack and ran away.

His stomach was full and he felt so warm and snug
that before he knew it he was asleep.

The old man hadn't been asleep
very long when he woke up.
Something was climbing
up the side of his cabin.
It sounded like a cat,
SCRATCH,
SCRATCH,
SCRATCH.

"Who's that?" the old man asked.
He lay still and listened,
and after a while he heard a voice say:

"*Tailypo, tailypo,*
all I want is my tailypo."

The scratching went on and on, and the old man began
to shiver and shake. Then he remembered his dogs.
He went to the door and called, "Here, here, here!"

The dogs came piling out from under the porch,
and with their noses to the ground they chased that thing
into the deep, big woods.

The old man pulled his covers tightly around him
and went back to sleep.

In the middle of the night he woke up again.
Now he heard something trying to get in
right above the cabin door.

"Who's that?" he called.
"And what do you want at this time of night
when all good folks should be in bed?"

He listened and he could hear it going,
SCRATCH, SCRATCH, SCRATCH.

Then he heard the voice say:

*"Tailypo, tailypo,
I'm coming to get my tailypo!"*

The old man was so scared he couldn't stand up. So he called
his dogs from his bed, "Uno, Ino, Cumptico-Calico.
Here, here, here!" And those dogs came bursting
around the corner of the cabin.

They caught up with that wild thing at the gate
and tore the whole fence down trying to get at it.
Then they chased it into the swamp.

At last all was quiet again. With a weary sigh, the man
went back to sleep.

Toward morning something down in the swamp
woke up the old man. First he thought it was the wind
blowing louder than usual. But when he listened again,
he heard that voice crying:

*"You know, and I know,
all I want is my tailypo."*

The old man called his dogs, "Here, here, here!
Uno, Ino, Cumptico-Calico!"

This time the dogs didn't come.

The old man ran outside into the moonlight
and called again,
"Here, dogs, here, here, here!"

But there was no trace of them. There was
just the sound of the wind blowing around the torn-down fence.
That thing had led the dogs way off into the swamp
and lost them.

Sadly the man went back inside the cabin
and shut and barred the door. Then he went back to bed.

Just before daylight the old man opened his eyes,
the way people do when they feel there's someone else
in the room. Something was stirring among the pots and pans.
Then something that sounded just like a cat began climbing up
the covers at the foot of the bed. The man listened
and heard it, SCRATCH, SCRATCH, SCRATCH.

He looked over the foot of his bed and saw two pointed ears.
Then he saw two big, round, fiery eyes staring at him.
The man wanted to call for help, but he was too scared.

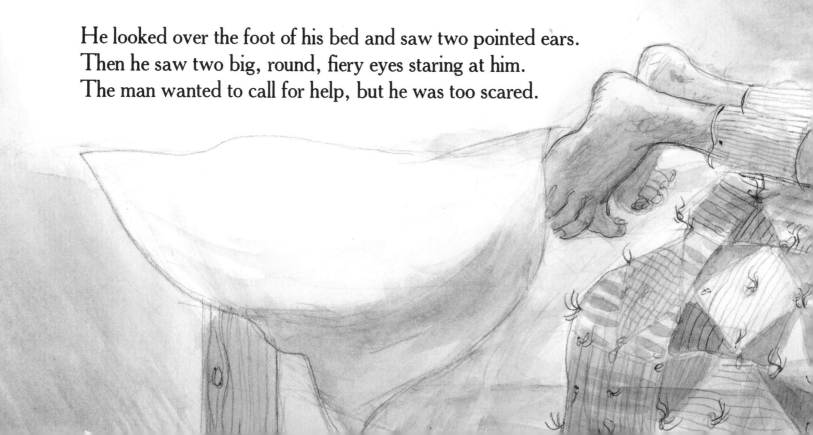

That thing kept creeping up until it was right next to the old man. Then it said in a low voice:

"*You know, and I know,*
that I'm here to get my tailypo."

The man sat up and pulled the covers
over his head. All at once he got his voice and said,
"I haven't got your tailypo!"

"Yes, you have," said the thing. "Yes, you have."
And it jumped on top of that man
and scratched everything to pieces.

Now there's nothing left of the old man's cabin
in the deep, big woods except the chimney.
But folks who live in the valley say
that when the moon shines and the wind blows,
you can hear a voice say:

"Tailypo, tailypo,
  now I've got
  my tailypo."